TEACHER
TROUBLE

Steve Barlow and Steve Skidmore

Illustrated by Alex Lopez

LONDON·SYDNEY

Franklin Watts
First published in Great Britain in 2017 by The Watts Publishing Group

Credits
Executive Editor: Adrian Cole
Design Manager: Peter Scoulding
Cover Designer: Cathryn Gilbert
Illustrations: Alex Lopez

HB ISBN 978 1 4451 5373 5
PB ISBN 978 1 4451 5375 9
Library ebook ISBN 978 1 4451 5374 2

Printed in China.

MIX
Paper from
responsible sources
FSC® C104740

FSC
www.fsc.org

Franklin Watts
An imprint of
Hachette Children's Group
Part of The Watts Publishing Group
Carmelite House
50 Victoria Embankment
London EC4Y 0DZ

An Hachette UK Company
www.hachette.co.uk

www.franklinwatts.co.uk

Lin

Danny

Sam

"What does he mean?" asked Lin.

Sam shook his head. "No idea."

14

"What sort of things?" asked Clogger.

"Garlic, silver chains, salt, a bottle of holy water..."

Clogger laughed. "Maybe he's a monster hunter! He's come to take away the freaks."

SPLURGE!

Danny, Lin and Sam were shocked.

"A monster hunter! What should we do?" asked Danny.

"What will he do to us?" asked Sam.

"I have an idea. We should ask him
if he is a monster hunter," said Lin.
"Are you mad?" hissed Danny.
"No. Come on," replied Lin.

"Hello. Can I help?" said Mr Hunter.

"We've heard a story... People say you are a monster hunter," said Lin.

23

24

25

"What are you doing?" screamed
the headteacher.

"There are monsters here!" said
Mr Hunter.

"You are the only monster here!"
replied the headteacher.

"Get out, now!"